Silent Dreams

Written by Dandi Daley Mackall

Illustrated by Karen A. Jerome

Dandi Mackall

For my husband, Joe, the love of my life and the answer to my dreams.
D. D. M.
For Robert Y. Larsen, with deep repect and appreciation.
K. A. J.

Text © 2003 by Dandi Daley Mackall
Illustrations © 2003 by Karen A. Jerome
Published in 2003 by Eerdmans Books for Young Readers
An imprint of Wm. B. Eerdmans Publishing Company
255 Jefferson S.E., Grand Rapids, Michigan 49503
P.O. Box 163, Cambridge CB3 9PU U.K.

Mackall, Dandi Daley.
Silent dreams / written by Dandi Daley Mackall ; illustrated by Karen Jerome.
p. cm.
Summary: Orphaned Camilla and her aunt, two of the many homeless persons in early twentieth-century America, forget their difficult lives when they go to the Saturday motion picture matinee. Includes an historical note on silent movies.

ISBN 0-8028-5200-9 (alk. paper)

[1. Homeless persons—Fiction. 2. Motion pictures—Fiction. 3. Orphans—Fiction.
4. Aunts—Fiction. 5. Stories in rhyme.] I. Jerome, Karen A., ill. II. Title.

PZ8.3.M179 Si 2002
[Fic]—dc21
2002021608

The illustrations were done in watercolor.
The display type was set in University Roman Bold.
The text type was set in Stone Informal.
Book design by Matthew Van Zomeren

*I*n the middle of the middle of a movie matinee
Sit Camilla and her auntie as on every Saturday.

Back in early 1900s both her folks had died of flu,
Leaving no one for Camilla but an aunt she barely knew.
So they found their way together, leaving more and more behind,
'Til one day it seemed Aunt's body just got up and left her mind.

On a Monday at Saint Vincent's stood Camilla and her aunt
In a long, cold line for supper at the back door south of Grant.
"Five more days," said Jake the Badger, as they reached the church's door.
Father Joe smiled at Camilla. "Take a loaf. Wish it were more."

In the flats down by the river in a soggy cardboard box
Slept Camilla and her auntie in a place where no one knocks.
In Camilla's dreams, her auntie talked and talked the whole night through.
In the morning Aunt was silent as the still and soundless dew.

"Four more days," said Toots on Tuesday, when they passed her on the street.
"Here's a nickel for your ticket. Valentino sure is sweet!"

"Here's a bit of scratch," said Jugman, when a blizzard came their way.

"For the shell game's going nicely. Three more days to Saturday!"

"Two more days, Aunt," called Camilla when her aunt refused to rise
On the Thursday when a film of fog first swallowed up the skies.
Auntie's eyes were like a blank screen when that Friday rolled around,
So Camilla searched for pennies at the local lost and found.

Friday night they begged on Fourth Street as the shoppers scurried by.

"Two more cents, Tom?" asked Camilla. Two-Time Tommy gave a sigh.

"Here's a cent from Fingers Freddy and another one from me."

(Auntie used to say pickpockets could be kind as kind could be.)

In the middle of the middle of a movie matinee,
Sat Camilla and her auntie as on every Saturday.
Auntie stared up at the blank screen as if begging for a tale,
While Camilla sat beside her and the house lights dimmed to pale.

All at once the shy piano rang with promises and pain,
And the music of the theater drowned the pounding of the rain.
In the dark her aunt's galoshes squeaked with toes that tapped the floor,
And to see her auntie swaying touched Camilla to the core.

Auntie frowned up at the villain, and his shadows splashed her cheek
As Camilla watched the lips move on those mouths that never speak.

On the screen flashed words unspoken, words Camilla could not read.
And she wondered, could her auntie — though there wasn't any need
For the next scene showed the heroine bound to hard, cold railroad tracks!
And the train kept drawing nearer, leaving no doubt as to facts.

As the villain stroked his mustache, Auntie cringed — Camilla jeered —
For an hour and twenty minutes when the whole world disappeared.

They both watched the show in silence; not a word passed in between,
While the handsome men and ladies danced across the silver screen.
Lost in thought and simple story as the hero saved the day,
Still Camilla knew what followed when the music ceased to play.

All at once the show was over and the theater screen went black.
Then the lights and tangled voices from the outside world rushed back.
"Thank you, Billy," said Camilla when the usher tipped his cap.
"Here's your shawl, Aunt." And Camilla neatly tied the tattered wrap.

Once outside, the dusk was dreary as they shuffled down the street,
Toward the stand of Boxcar Betty and the man who had no feet.
"If we hurry we'll make vespers!" But her aunt had ceased to hear,
For already nothing mattered but the music in her ear.

As they walked past Boxcar Betty, Betty nodded her hello.
"How's your aunt?" asked Fingers Freddy. "Bet she liked the picture show."
"Right as rain," replied Camilla. But her aunt stared straight ahead.
"We'll be waiting by the river just past dark," the Jugman said.

Near the shacks down by the river where the hard-luck people stay,
They are gathered by the blazing fires to hear of Saturday.
Fingers Freddy plays a washboard. Toots and Jugman hum a tune.
Boxcar Betty smokes a cigar. Two-time Tommy plays the spoon.

Then Camilla takes a grand bow. And with all her soul and heart,
To the eager down-and-outers she begins to play each part.
Jake's and Freddy's eyes grow giant, Boxcar Betty screams out loud,
When Camilla as the villain storms her way into the crowd!

When the show is not quite over, from the crowd there comes a chant,
And before she turns around Camilla knows that it's her aunt,
In a voice too long forsaken, Auntie cries, "Encore! Encore!"
And just as in Camilla's dreams, her auntie shines once more.

How Camilla knows what's coming, she will never understand,
But she reaches out to Auntie, and she takes the bony hand.
Then she asks, "Who'll be my heroine?" Auntie answers low, "I will."
And a motion picture miracle unfolds upon that hill.

For the last act of the story plays to flickering firelight,
As Camilla and her auntie break the silence of the night.

*I*n the middle of the middle of a movie matinee
Sit Camilla and her auntie as on every Saturday.
In the silence of the story and the drama of the dream,
Live Camilla and her auntie on the bright side of the screen.

About Silent Dreams

When I was 8 years old, my parents took my sister and me on a real vacation, to stay in a real hotel in New York City. I'm sure we must have visited the Empire State Building, Broadway, and museums, but what I remember most was my first glimpse of homeless people.

On one street corner, dressed in rags, stood a stocky woman smoking a cigar. I stopped and must have stared open-mouthed until the old woman blew smoke in my face. I heard my dad's footsteps behind me. But instead of dragging me away to safety, Dad stopped too. "Dandi," he said, "don't be rude. Introduce yourself."

I did, and the woman came to life. "I'm Boxcar Betty," she said, sticking out the dirtiest hand I'd ever seen — I shook it — "and I ride the rails." For the next hour, our new friend told us stories about living a hobo's life, tramping, and making it on the streets of the city and in the backwoods of middle America.

On our way back to our hotel, I didn't see the skyscrapers or window displays. I was too caught up — waving to a man playing the shell game down a back alley, taking an ad flyer on 42nd Street from a man who had no feet, and seeing for the first time Boxcar Betty's world.

— *Dandi Daley Mackall*

Silent Motion Picture Era

For many Americans, the years of silent movies (about 1900-1930) were hard times. Soldiers fought on a faraway continent in World War I. Flu epidemics killed hundreds of thousands, panicking entire cities and leaving homeless orphans to live on the streets.

Silent films entertained the world until the late 1920s, when "talkies," movies with sound, took over. Characters acted out the story, but mouthed the words or dialogue. Without the technology to produce sound along with the picture, producers relied on printed words flashed on the screen from time to time throughout the film. For music, piano players often banged out accompaniment right in the local theater — galloping music, romantic or sad songs, or villainous pounding to signal danger.

Some silent motion pictures, like "The Perils of Pauline" or "A Dangerous Adventure," appeared in a series of fifteen episodes. Each film ended with a "cliffhanger" — sometimes the heroine actually was dangling from a steep cliff. This lured movie-goers back each week for more adventure.

Even though many people, even children, were so poor they were forced to live on the streets, most went to the movies once a week or more. Silent movies offered more than entertainment. For an hour or two each Saturday, the movie matinee brought escape.

Glossary

Boxcar – One of the cars in a freight train that hobos might hop onto for a free ride or temporary shelter

Cliffhanger – An adventure or melodrama presented in a series of installments that each end in suspense

Flats – A level area of land

Heroine – Central female character in a dramatic work

Hobo – A homeless person who wanders from place to place

Jugman – Slang for someone who robs banks

Local lost and found – Any public place where someone may have dropped a coin or two

Mark – A victim or prospective victim of a swindle

Pickpockets – Crooks who could steal a wallet or a watch without the "mark" realizing it

Scratch – Slang for money

Shell game – A gambling game, usually played on the streets by tricksters who could pretend to hide a ball under one of the three walnet shells and let the "mark" guess where it was

Two-time – To double-cross or betray

Valentino – Rudolf Valentino, one the most famous and dashing romantic stars of the silent movies

Villain – An evil person in a story or play